For James Alexander Egan S. I.

For Marcus and Porridge N. R.

First published in 1995

3 5 7 9 10 8 6 4 2

First published in the United Kingdom in 1995 by
Hutchinson Children's Books, Random House UK Limited
20 Vauxhall Bridge Road, London SW1V 2SA

Random House Australia (Pty) Limited, 20 Alfred Street, Milsons Point, Sydney
New South Wales 2061, Australia

Random House New Zealand Limited, 18 Poland Road, Glenfield
Auckland 10, New Zealand

Random House South Africa (Pty) Limited, PO Box 337, Bergvlei, South Africa

Random House UK Limited Reg. No. 954009

A CIP catalogue record for this book is available from the British Library

ISBN: 0 09 176602 8

Printed in Hong Kong

Something for
James

Shirley Isherwood
& Neil Reed

HUTCHINSON
London Sydney Aukland Johannesburg

One day, something arrived in a brown paper bag for James.
Elephant found it on the doorstep. It was a large brown paper bag,
and the top was twisted tightly round so that Elephant couldn't see
what was inside. But she heard a rustling sound, and then a hiccup.

Elephant put on her spectacles, and read the label which was
tied to the bag. 'Something for James,' she read.

James had gone for a walk with Winston. They went for a walk
together every day.

Elephant sat on the doorstep, and waited as patiently as she could. Something in the bag sighed.

'Oh my,' said Elephant and, very carefully, she opened the bag and peeped inside.

Two great dark eyes gazed back at her for a moment, and she caught a glimpse of two long soft ears.

'Are you a rabbit, dear?' asked Elephant. The soft fluffy ears certainly looked like rabbit ears.

Whoever was in the bag didn't answer.

'Perhaps you're a puppy, dear,' said Elephant, for she could see a nice round tummy. But whoever was in the bag wasn't a puppy. Winston was a puppy, and he barked and scampered about. Whoever was in the bag sat quietly and didn't stir.

Elephant closed the bag, and put it carefully back on the doorstep. Then she set off down the lane to find James and Winston. 'Something in a bag for James,' she said as she went, so that she would remember everything. 'Long soft ears, big dark eyes, nice round tummy. Hiccupping and sighing.'

Then, when she had almost reached the bend in the lane, she suddenly thought, Suppose the something in the bag is a fierce something. Sometimes, fierce things lie quietly, and then *pounce!*

She hurried on as quickly as she could, and was very glad when she heard James and Winston cry 'Turn left!', and saw them come marching into sight.

Elephant ran to meet them.

'Hurry home at once!' she said. 'There's something sighing in a brown paper bag. It might be a terrible fierce pouncer!'

'A what?' said James.

Elephant tried to gather her thoughts together, but before she could tell James about the great dark eyes, the nice round tummy, and the hiccups, Winston had set off down the lane, barking loudly.

'I'll get that terrible fierce pouncer!' he said, as he ran. James and Elephant ran after him, but by the time they reached the house, Winston had picked up the bag and was racing round and round the garden. Elephant and James caught up with him by the fish pond.

Winston was very pleased with himself, and dropped the bag at James's feet. At once, the bag rolled down the sloping lawn and into the reeds that grew by the edge of the water.

'Oh, my!' said Elephant.

The bottom of the bag was quite wet. As Elephant lifted it out with her long trunk, the paper tore and the tip of a soft grey paw with pink velvety pads peeped out.

'It isn't a terrible fierce pouncer,' said James, as he and Winston followed Elephant to the house.

Winston said nothing, but he thought, Well, it *might* have been.

Elephant put the bag on the rug to dry. Something in the bag sighed and then sneezed.

James opened the bag and peeped inside. 'Please come out,' he said, but something just covered its eyes with its ears and curled into a ball.

Elephant put the tip of her trunk into the bag, but something just rustled about in a worried manner.

'He really should come out,' said Elephant. 'His paws are quite damp.'

James went upstairs to look for Bear, and found him asleep on the windowsill.

'Bear,' said James, 'something has arrived in a bag, and he won't come out.'

Bear woke up at once. 'How exciting!' he said, as he jumped from the windowsill.

'How mysterious,' he said, as he padded down the stairs.

'How extraordinary,' said Bear, as he looked at the bag which lay rustling on the rug.

'We thought that it might have been a terrible fierce pouncer,' said Winston.

'Terrible fierce pouncers don't arrive in brown paper bags,' said Bear. He was very old, and knew almost everything.

He put his paw into the bag, and the worried rustling stopped at once. Bear's paw had the comforting smell of biscuits and cocoa.

Two long ears appeared from the bag, and two dark eyes, followed by the round tummy and soft grey paws with velvety pink pads.

James, Winston, Elephant and Bear were very pleased to see him.

'But what is he?' James whispered to Bear.

'He's a Something,' said Bear. 'It says so on the label. "Something for James."'

Elephant brought Something a mug of warm milk. Something drank it in one go, and then went back into his bag.

'Better leave him to settle in his own time,' said Bear, and went back to his windowsill.

James, Elephant and Winston went to bed. Winston slept
at James's feet, and Elephant slept by his pillow, as they had
always done. Everyone slept soundly, but woke up some
time later to hear a rustling sound. Opening the bedroom
door, they saw Something making his way up the stairs,
dragging his paper bag behind him.

Everyone went quickly back to bed so that he wouldn't be alarmed by the sight of the faces looking at him through the banisters.

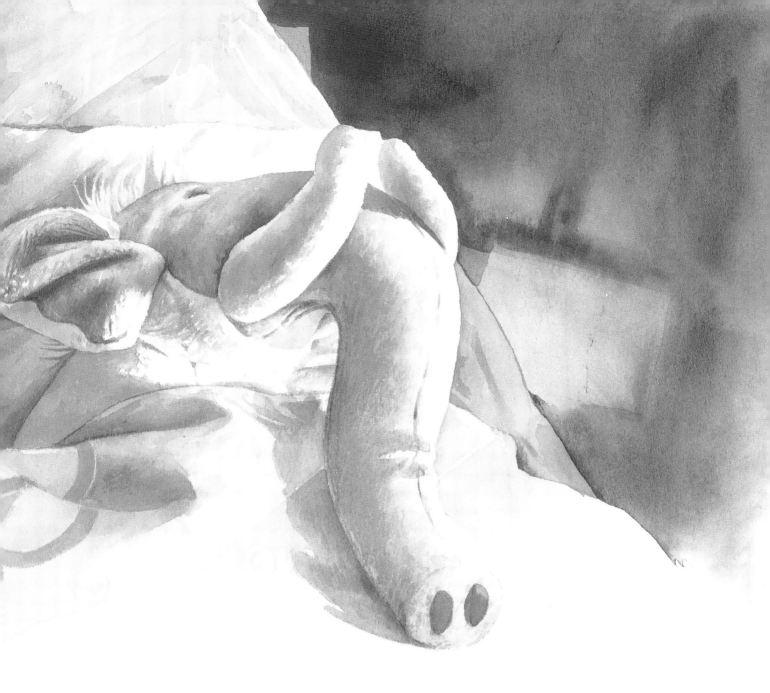

Soon after, James felt Something creep quietly on to the pillow.
'Good night, Something,' said James, and heard him give a
happy sigh as he snuggled down under the blanket.
One of his soft grey paws was still quite damp.